Peace In Our Land

Children Celebrating Diversity

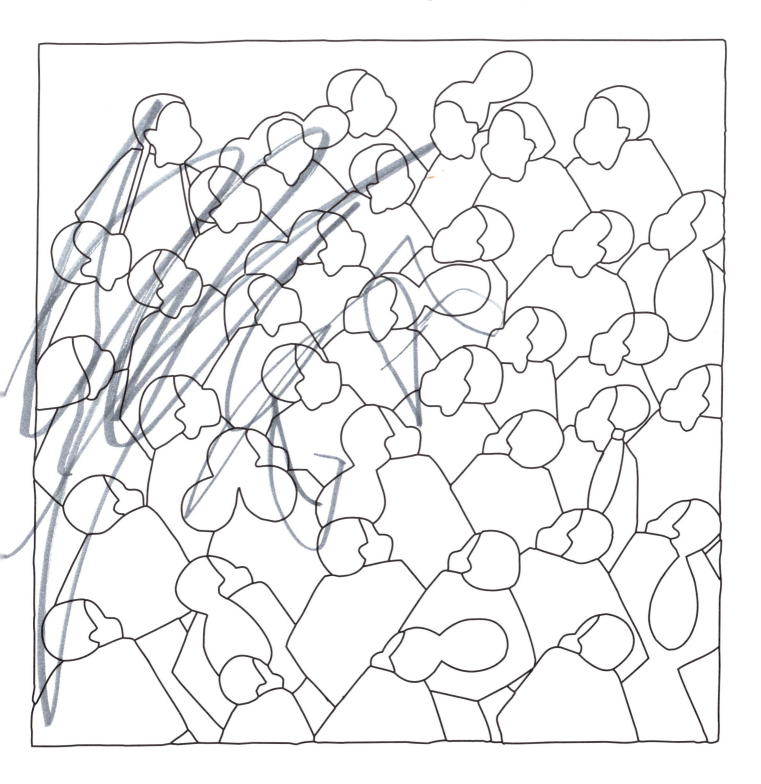

COLOR YOUR WORLD

THIS BOOK IS DEDICATED to all who lost their lives to events of September 11th, to their families and friends, and to all those who have worked to put it all back together again—including all of us.

This is dedicated to children everywhere. May we guide them to remember how special they are, to honor their differences and remind them that they can change their own lives and the world by using the power of their minds.

We change the world by changing ourselves.

Let us acknowledge what unites us and celebrate our differences.

Thank you to the many good friends who added their special talents to this package

"I Plant A Seed" (poem) – Read by Tati Houston

"A World Of Difference"
Background Vocals: Bunny Hull & Anindo • Guitar: Corky James

"I Believe In Myself"

"Peace In Our Land"
African drums: Anindo • Peace Choir: Keechar Broadnax,
Brooke Williams, Thelma Houston, Laythan Armor, Lorraine Fields, Anindo

"A Smile Is A Smile"
Trombone: Eric Jorgenson • Brushes: Jeff Hull

"The Truth About Friendship" – Read by Elayn Taylor

"Family"
Bunny Hull & Laythan Armor

"Love Comes In Every Color"

"Thankful"

Production, arranging, keyboards,
programming and lead vocals by Bunny Hull

**Special Thanks to Dr. David J. Walker
and an unidentified child from South Africa**

Lyrics available at www.brassheartmusic.com

Book design & layout by James Suelflow Design

All Songs Music & Lyrics by Bunny Hull © 2001, 2002 BrassHeart Music
except "Family" by Bunny Hull & Laythan Armor © 2002 BrassHeart Music/Leigharm Music

Content and story written by Bunny Hull © 2002 BrassHeart Music

Cover Art "Harmony" and Illustrations by Synthia Saint James © 2002

I plant a seed of love,
And know that seed will grow;

That love will always find me,
Wherever I may go.

I plant a seed of peace,
Of friendship kind and true;

And know peace grows
with every seed I plant
For me and you.

PEACE BEGINS WITH ME.

Iᴛ's ᴀ ʙɪɢ ʙᴇᴀᴜᴛɪꜰᴜʟ ᴡᴏʀʟᴅ. Look at a globe or a map. There are many lands, languages, religions cultures and many, many people. Is there someplace you'd like to visit someday? Do you know what is different about us? Do you know what is the same? Do you know what connects us?

Just by exploring our own worlds and talking to our schoolmates, our families and friends we can learn the answers to all these questions. Each one of us is special. Our differences are beautiful. Our colors are beautiful... just like a rainbow.

Sɪɴɢ ᴀʟᴏɴɢ ᴡɪᴛʜ "A Wᴏʀʟᴅ ᴏꜰ Dɪꜰꜰᴇʀᴇɴᴄᴇ."

Do you know what country your family originally came from?

Where is it? _____

What language do they speak there? _____

Can you teach your friends to say a word in that language?

What word? _____

What kind of special food do they cook in the country your family is from?

_____

Name four of your friends. Where are they from, and what language do they speak? What is something they eat there?

	Name	Country	Language	Food
1.	_____	_____	_____	_____
2.	_____	_____	_____	_____
3.	_____	_____	_____	_____
4.	_____	_____	_____	_____

ACTIVITY #1 *(answers on the last page)*

Can you draw a line to match the country with the food you can eat there?

Japan	Spaghetti
America	Enchiladas
Italy	Hamburger
Mexico	Wonton
China	Sushi
Kenya	Sukumawiki

I ENJOY LEARNING ABOUT OTHERS.

YOU ARE SPECIAL! Did you know that there is only one of you? You have your own fingerprints, your own voice, your own special talents and you and only you make your own choices about everything?

What is your favorite color?_____

What is your favorite music? _____

What is your favorite food? _____

Who is your favorite friend? _____

Who do you love? _____

Ask your friends and family these same questions. Each person will have a different answer. Every person in the world will have a different answer. WE ARE ALL UNIQUE!

I BELIEVE IN MYSELF AND OTHERS.

ACTIVITY #2 *(answers are on the last page)*

What are some of the things that are THE SAME about us even though we might be from a different part of the world or speak another language?

Draw a line to match these things that we might have in common with others.

Something we can do with our face	A hug from someone we love
Something we like to do	A beautiful sunset
Something we like to eat	Ourselves and each other
Something we like to look at	Ice cream
Something we like to get	Disneyland
Something we believe in	Listen to music
Someplace we'd like to go	Smile

ACTIVITY #3 *(answers are on the last page)*

What are some of the things WE FEEL THAT ARE THE SAME?

Draw a line to match these feelings that we might have in common with others.

When we are sad	We smile and laugh
When we are happy	We feel extra creative
When we are afraid	We feel good inside
When we give love	We feel proud
When we accomplish something	We believe everything will be all right
When we feel inspired	We cry

When we can see how much we are the same, and also celebrate our differences, then we can see how great we all really are.

WE'RE ALL CONNECTED.

Sing along with "Peace In Our Land"

We are connected you and I;
Over the earth and under the sky.

We are the same under our skin;
We may be different without, but we're the same within.

We are the same within...

And there is love for you and me;
Let there be hope and harmony.

Let there be harmony...

Let there be peace
in our land;

Let there be love,
let us understand.

Let there be peace,
all over the world;

Let there be love,
let there be happiness...

Brothers and sisters all are we;
Who share one world who share one dream.

It's up to us to plant the seed;
It's up to us we must believe.

We must believe...

And do our part, you and me;
Do it together in harmony.

Let there be harmony...

Let there be peace in our land;
Let there be love, let us understand.

Let there be peace, all over the world;
Let there be love, let there be happiness...

Put your two fingers up, raise your right hand
Everybody let's have peace in our land

Divided we fall, united we stand;
Everybody let's have peace in our land...

Say Peace; "Peace!"
Say Peace; "Peace!"
Say Peace; "Peace!"
Let's have peace in our land... *(repeat)*

Let there be peace in our land;
Let there be love, let us understand.

Let there be peace, all over the world;
Let there be love, let there be happiness...

Say a prayer for peace, for every nation;
Say a prayer for peace;
Let there be peace in our land.

Say a prayer for peace, for all of creation
Say a prayer for peace;
Let there be peace in our land...

Say a prayer for peace, for every nation;
Say a prayer for peace;
Let there be peace in our land.

Pᴇᴏᴘʟᴇ ᴘʀᴀʏ ɪɴ ᴛʜᴇɪʀ ᴏᴡɴ ᴡᴀʏs ᴀʟʟ ᴏᴠᴇʀ ᴛʜᴇ ᴡᴏʀʟᴅ. No matter how different the words of a prayer might be, a prayer is said to cause something good.

There are many different religions. Some people may not be a part of a religion or pray at all. That's okay too! Everyone has their own beliefs and we celebrate our freedom of choice.

Do you have a religion?

What religion are you? _____

Ask three of your friends about their religion.

My friends	Their religion
1. _____	_____
2. _____	_____
3. _____	_____

Aᴄᴛɪᴠɪᴛʏ #4 *(answers are on the last page)*

Your friends might be one of these religions. Can you draw a line and match each religion to the book it teaches from?

Jewish	The Koran
Muslim	The Bahagvad Gita
Buddhist	The Bible
Hindu	The Bible, The Torah, The Koran & others
Christian	The Lotus Sutra
New Thought	The Torah

I ʜᴀᴠᴇ ꜰᴀɪᴛʜ.

There are many more religions, and even more languages. Do you know how you can speak to someone even if you don't know their language?

Sing along with "A Smile Is A Smile Is A Smile"

Oh you may not know how to say hello
In Spain or France or Tokyo...

**But if you've got a face, you can make your case,
'Cause a smile is a smile is a smile...**

Oh you may be brave, or you may be shy;
Afraid to speak and don't know why;

Well just curl your mouth, and let your fears go south,
'Cause a smile is a smile is a smile...

A smile doesn't need a language;
A smile only needs a heart,
To give direction to your face,
So you can make the sun shine all over the place...

So when things get tough, wanna shed a tear;
Just show your teeth from ear to ear...

Doesn't cost a thing, so go on and grin;
Make somebody's day worthwhile

'Cause a smile is a smile is a smile!

The Truth About Friendship

IT WAS ANDRE'S VERY FIRST DAY in second grade, and he was kind of scared. He had recently moved to Los Angeles from a small town in France, but his English was really good. He didn't even have an accent. Andre didn't know anybody at his new school. His mom walked him to the classroom, gave him a kiss on the cheek, and waved good-bye. I don't think Andre said two words that morning. He just watched and listened.

At lunch everybody made a beeline for the basketball court, leaving Andre behind. He made his way out on to the playground taking his time, noticing that some of the other kids were turned around pointing at him as they walked ahead. Tati decided to stay behind walking beside Andre.

"How come you're in a wheelchair?" asked Tati.

"I have a condition that makes my legs too weak to walk."

"Oh," said Tati. "Does it hurt?"

"No, not at all."

"That's good," said Tati. "I never met anyone in a wheelchair before. Can I push it?"

"Okay," said Andre, and they made their way together out onto the playground to have lunch.

Andre and Tati became fast friends that day. Andre told Tati about France, and Tati told Andre her mother and father were from Mexico, and her grandmother lived with them.

"Me too," he said. "It's my mother, my grandmother, me, and my little brother, Pierre. My father doesn't live with us anymore."

"I have a little brother too," said Tati.

They talked and talked. They talked about what foods they liked, their favorite music... Andre told Tati his family was Jewish, and Tati said her family was Catholic.

They were very deep in conversation when they noticed that the kids that had been pointing at Andre earlier were yelling for help. Something was wrong! One of the guys, Rufus, was on the ground crying. He had turned his ankle so badly playing basketball that he couldn't walk.

Andre quickly wheeled his chair over to where the boys were, Tati by his side. "Can I help?" he said.

"I can't walk," said Rufus, "but I don't think you can help."

"Sit on my lap, Rufus, and I'll wheel you back to the office."

"Oh!" said Rufus, and stopped crying. "Won't that hurt you?"

"Oh, no," said Andre.

So the other kids helped Rufus up onto Andre's lap, and all the kids, Tati, Francis, Ali, Keechar, Jay-Jay, and the others crowded around the chair to push Rufus and Andre back to the office where the school nurse came out to help.

"Thank you Andre," said Rufus, sniffling a little.

"No problem!" said Andre.

"Tomorrow," said Rufus, "will you come out and play with us?"

Andre got a hu-u-u-ge smile on his face. "That would be great!"

That day was a special day because everyone learned something. Andre felt really good about helping someone—it made him feel good inside! And the rest of the kids no longer thought of Andre as different. He was just one of the guys.

Tati and Rufus found out that being in a wheelchair didn't hurt. And, just by talking with Andre, Tati found out that even though someone comes from a different country, speaks a different language and has a different religion, that you can have more in common with them than you'd ever imagine.

"Isn't it great making new friends?" asked Tati. "If people all over the world learned about each other. There would be peace in every land."

"That's the truth," said Andre. "It makes the world seem very small."

And ever since that day, Tati, Andre, and Rufus were absolutely inseparable!

The world is made of different kinds of families. Not everyone has both a mother and father in their family, and that's okay. Some people have big families and some have small families.

A family is made of people you love and care about and who care about you. It can include friends too!

Who makes up your family?

_____   _____

_____   _____

_____   _____

Listen to "Family" and draw your family.

LOVE MAKES THE WORLD BEAUTIFUL.

WE ALL SHARE the same earth, we all breathe the same air, we all feel the warmth of the same sun...and we all feel love.

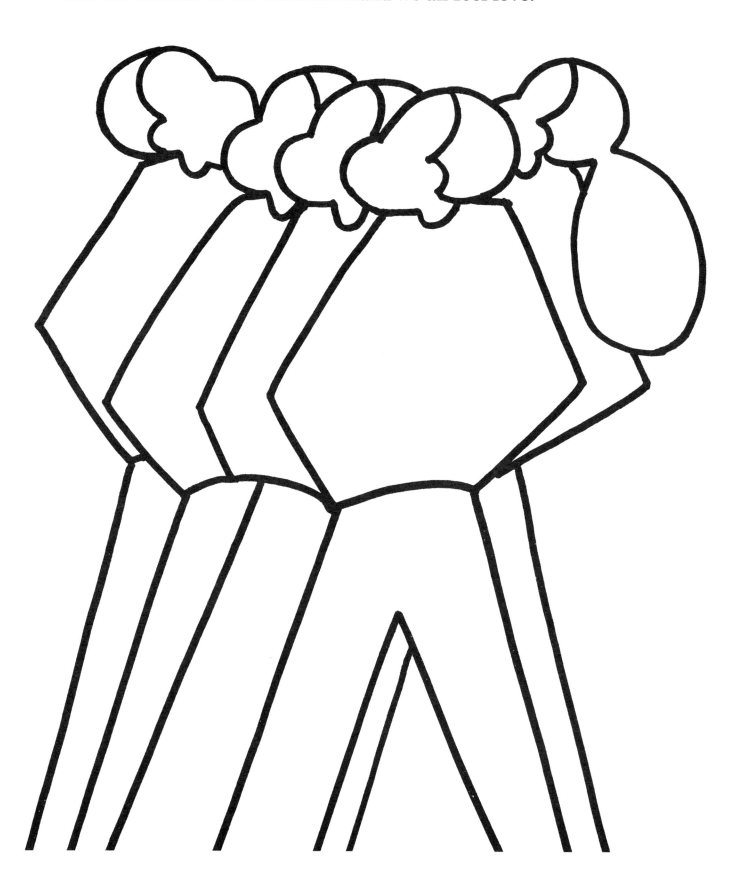

LOVE COMES IN EVERY COLOR.

Love makes the world a better place!

Activity #5 *(answers are on the last page)*

Circle the ways you can help to make the world a better place.

a) Doing well in school

b) Listening when someone talks to me

c) Being jealous of someone else

d) Being happy for someone else

e) Not sharing what I have with others

f) Telling someone I love them

g) Being thankful for my friends

h) By being myself

Activity #6 *(answers are on the last page)*

Circle the simple acts of kindness that you can practice?

a) Taking care of my neighborhood

b) Helping someone who needs help

c) Being stubborn

d) Bringing a flower to my teacher

e) Smiling at someone new at school or in my neighborhood

f) Making fun of someone

g) Sharing my lunch

"A Drop of Peace" *This is fun! Try it...*

You need a big clear glass bowl filled with water, and some yellow and red food coloring for this activity.

Did you know that one small drop of peace spreads into the whole world? Try dropping a drop of red food coloring in a clear bowl of water. When you drop it in, say something you will do for peace. Watch it spread! See how it reaches out? Ask a friend to add a yellow drop, and let them say something they will do for peace. See how it spreads too, and blends with the other one? If everyone adds one small drop of peace to the world they will all add together to create a beautiful ocean of peace!

I am a peacemaker!

Make peace in your world. When we make ourselves better, we make the whole world better. "Let there be peace in our land."

Answers to Activity #1

Japan —————————————— Sushi

America —————————————— Hamburger

Italy —————————————— Spaghetti

Mexico —————————————— Enchiladas

China —————————————— Wonton

Kenya —————————————— Sukumawiki
(Collard greens)

Answers to Activity #2

Something we do with our face ————— Smile

Something we like to do ————— Listen to music

Something we like to eat ————— Ice Cream

Something we like to look at————— A beautiful sunset

Something we like to get ————— A hug from someone we love

Something we believe in————— Ourselves and each other

Someplace we'd like to go ————— Disneyland

Answers to Activity #3

When we are sad————— We cry

When we are happy ————— We smile & laugh

When we are afraid ————— We believe everything will be alright

When we give love ————— We feel good inside

When we accomplish something ————— We feel proud

When we feel inspired ————— We feel extra creative

Answers to Activity #4

Jewish —————————————— The Torah

Muslim —————————————— The Koran

Buddhist —————————————— The Lotus Sutra

Hindu —————————————— The Bahagvad Gita

Christian —————————————— The Bible

New Thought—————————————— The Bible, The Torah, The Koran and others

Answers to Activity #5

a) Doing well in school   **b)** Listening when someone talks   **d)** Being happy for someone else

f) Telling someone I love them   **g)** Being thankful for my friends   **h)** By being myself

Answers to Activity #6

a) Taking care of my neighborhood   **b)** Helping someone who needs help

d) bringing a flower to my teacher   **e)** smiling at someone new at school or in my neighborhood

g) sharing my lunch